Ghosts and Goose Bumps
Poems to Chill Your Bones

How happy am I when I crawl into bed—
A rattlesnake hisses a tune at my head,
A gay little centipede, all without fear,
Crawls over my pillow and into my ear.

Traditional

A Random House PICTUREBACK®

ACKNOWLEDGMENTS

Grateful acknowledgment is made to the following for permission to reprint the copyrighted material below: BookStop Literary Agency for: "Monster Stew" by Judith Kinter. Copyright © 1989 by Judith Kinter. "Ghost Bus" by Joe Wayman. Copyright © 1989 by Joe Wayman. Reprinted by permission of BookStop Literary Agency for the authors. Laura Cecil for "The Bogus Boo" by James Reeves. Copyright James Reeves. Reprinted by permission of The James Reeves Estate. J. M. Dent & Sons, Ltd., for excerpt from "Uncle James" by Margaret Mahy from THE FIRST MARGARET MAHY STORYBOOK. Doubleday, Inc., for "The Cemetery Stones" from THE MIST MEN AND OTHER POEMS by George Mendoza and "The Bat" from THE COLLECTED POEMS OF THEODORE ROETHKE. Used by permission of Doubleday, a division of Bantam, Doubleday, Dell Publishing Group, Inc. British rights for "The Bat" were granted by Faber & Faber, Ltd. Samuel Exler for "A Magic Chant." Copyright © 1989 by Samuel Exler. Reprinted by permission of the author. Farrar, Straus and Giroux, Inc., for "Pumpkin" from MORE SMALL POEMS by Valerie Worth. Copyright © 1976 by Valerie Worth. Reprinted by permission of Farrar, Straus and Giroux, Inc. Greenwillow Books, a division of William Morrow & Company, for: "Skeleton Parade" from IT'S HALLOWEEN by Jack Prelutsky. Copyright © 1977 by Jack Prelutsky. "When I'm Very Nearly Sleeping" from WHEN MY PARENTS THINK I'M SLEEPING by Jack Prelutsky. Copyright © 1985 by Jack Prelutsky. Harper & Row, Publishers, Inc., for "The Witches' Ride" from THE ROSE ON MY CAKE by Karla Kuskin. Copyright © 1964 by Karla Kuskin. Reprinted by permission of Harper & Row, Publishers, Inc. Bobbi Katz for "Let's Be Spooky." Copyright © 1989 by Random House, Inc. J. Patrick Lewis for "The Owl" and "Your Shadow Says." Copyright © 1989 by J. Patrick Lewis. Used by permission of the author. Shelagh McGee for excerpt from "Wanted—a Witch's Cat" from WHAT WITCHES DO. Random House, Inc., Happy House Group, for excerpt from "Who Lives in This Haunted House?" by Bobbi Katz. Copyright © 1989 by Random House, Inc. Marian Reiner for "Look at That!" from SEE MY LOVELY POISON IVY by Lilian Moore. Copyright © 1975 by Lilian Moore. Reprinted by permission of Marian Reiner for the author. Scholastic, Inc., for "Johnny Drew a Monster" and "Teeny, Tiny Ghost" from SPOOKY RHYMES AND RIDDLES by Lilian Moore. Copyright © 1972 by Lilian Moore. Viking Penguin, Inc., for "Strange Tree" from UNDER THE TREE by Elizabeth Madox Roberts. Copyright 1922 by B. W. Huebsch, Inc. Copyright renewed 1950 by Ivor S. Roberts. Copyright 1930 by The Viking Press, Inc. Copyright renewed 1958 by Ivor S. Roberts and The Viking Press, Inc. All rights reserved. Reprinted by permission of Viking Penguin, a division of Penguin Books USA, Inc.

Library of Congress Cataloging-in-Publication Data
Ghosts and goose bumps: poems to chill your bones / selected by Bobbi Katz ; illustrated by Deborah Kogan Ray.   p.   cm— (A Random House pictureback) Summary: Scary poems by a variety of notable poets. ISBN 0-679-80372-6. (trade)— ISBN 0-679-90372-0 (lib. bdg.) 1. Supernatural—Juvenile poetry.   2. Children's poetry, American.   3. Children's poetry, English.   [1. Supernatural—Poetry.   2. Halloween—Poetry.   3. American poetry—Collections.   4. English poetry— Collections.]   I. Katz, Bobbi.   II. Ray Kogan, Deborah 1945– ill. PS595.S94S76 1990 89-37134 811'.00809282—dc20 CIP AC

Manufactured in the United States of America   4 5 6 7 8 9 10

Ghosts and Goose Bumps
Poems to Chill Your Bones

Selected by Bobbi Katz

Illustrated by Deborah Kogan Ray

Random House ⌂ New York

An Invitation

Let's be spooky. Let's have fun!
We'll scare ourselves before we're done
with ghosts and goblins — winds that howl —
things that fly and things that prowl.
We'll talk about such creepy stuff
until we both get scared enough
to hear things that we cannot see
and see things that just cannot be.
Let's be spooky — you and me.

Bobbi Katz

Your Shadow Says

I am you
but bigger than you
and longer than you
and darker than you

You are me
but smaller than me
and shorter than me
and afraid of me

J. Patrick Lewis

Autumn Ghost Sounds

When the moon
rides high,
up overhead—
and I am snug
and warm,
in bed—
in the autumn dark
the ghosts move 'round,
making their
mournful,
moaning sound.

I listen to know
when the ghosts
go by.
I hear a wail,
and I hear a sigh.

But I can't quite tell
which I hear
the most—
the wind,
or the wail
of some passing ghost.

Anonymous

Ghost Bus

Underneath the lamppost,
In the middle of the night,
A ghost bus makes a silent stop,
A strange and fearful sight.

At the bus stop at your corner,
Something big and green climbed down.
It's looking for your bedroom,
And it has searched all over town.

You thought it couldn't find you,
That you were safe and you were sound.
You thought that you could hide,
Where you never could be found.

But now it's almost here,
You know it loves the dark of night.
There's only one thing you can do,
Quick! Turn on the light!

Whew!

Joe Wayman

GHOSTS ON BOARD

Igga bigga, Hunka bunka, Dinka danka doo.

A Magic Chant

If in the dark you're frightened,
Here's all you have to do.
Say: Igga bigga,
Hunka bunka,
Dinka danka doo.

These words give you protection
From ghosts—and witches, too.
Say: Igga bigga,
Hunka bunka,
Dinka danka doo.

So if at night a monster
Should whisper, "I'll get you,"
Yell: Igga bigga,
Hunka bunka,
Dinka danka doo.

Samuel Exler

Johnny Drew a Monster

Johnny drew a monster.
The monster chased him.
Just in time
Johnny erased him.

Lilian Moore

The Bogus-Boo

The Bogus-boo
Is a creature who
Comes out at night—and why?
He likes the air;
He likes to scare
The nervous passer-by.

He has two wings,
Pathetic things,
With which he cannot fly.
His tusks look fierce,
Yet could not pierce
The merest butterfly.

He has six ears,
But what he hears
Is very faint and small;
And with the claws
On his eight paws
He cannot scratch at all.

He looks so wise
With his owl-eyes,
His aspect grim and ghoulish.
But truth to tell
He sees not well
And is distinctly foolish.

This Bogus-boo,
What can he do
But huffle in the dark?
So don't take fright;
He has no bite
And very little bark.

James Reeves

Uncle James

My Uncle James
Was a terrible man.
He cooked his wife
In the frying pan.

She's far too tender
To bake or boil!
He cooked her up
In peanut oil.

But sometime later—
A month or more—
There came a knock
On my uncle's door.

A great green devil
Was standing there.
He caught my uncle
By the hair.

"Are you the uncle
That cooked his wife,
And leads such a terribly
Wicked life?"

My uncle yowled
Like an old tom cat,
But the devil took him,
For all of that.

Oh, take a tip
From my Uncle James!
Don't throw stones
And don't call names.

Just be as good
As ever you can—
And never cook aunts
In a frying pan!

Margaret Mahy

Strange Tree

Away beyond the Jarboe house
I saw a different kind of tree.
Its trunk was old and large and bent,
And I could feel it look at me.

The road was going on and on
Beyond to reach some other place.
I saw a tree that looked at me
And yet it did not have a face.

It looked at me with all its limbs;
It looked at me with all its bark.
The yellow wrinkles on its sides
Were bent and dark.

And then I ran to get away,
But when I stopped to turn and see,
The tree was bending to the side
And leaning out to look at me.

Elizabeth Madox Roberts

Teeny Tiny Ghost

A teeny, tiny ghost
no bigger than a mouse
at most,
lived in a great big house.

It's hard to haunt
a great big house
when you're a teeny, tiny ghost
no bigger than a mouse
at most.

He did what he could do.

So every dark and stormy night
the kind that shakes the house with fright—
if you stood still and listened right,
you'd hear a
teeny
tiny

BOO!

Lilian Moore

Who Lives in This Haunted House?

Who lives in this haunted house?
"I do! I do!" says the mouse.
"See my aunts and all my cousins
scamper through it by the dozens."
Who else might be living here?
"Spiders, spiders, yes my dear!
Our webs grow bigger by the day.
No broom or mop sweeps them away."

Who likes this haunted house the *most*?
"I do! I do!" says the ghost.
"I can float from room to room,
having fun while spreading gloom.
This haunted house has stairs that creak.
Windows rattle. Hinges squeak.
It's such a lovely place to be
for someone who's a ghost like me!"

Bobbi Katz

The Tomcat

At midnight in the alley
A Tomcat comes to wail,
And he chants the hate of a million years
As he swings his snaky tail.

He twists and crouches and capers
And bares his curved sharp claws,
And he sings to the stars of the jungle nights,
Ere cities were, or laws.

He will lie on a rug tomorrow
And lick his silky fur,
And veil the brute in his yellow eyes
And play he's tame, and purr.

But at midnight in the alley
He will crouch again and wail,
And beat the time for his demon's song,
With the swing of his demon's tail.

Don Marquis

Queen Nefertiti

Spin a coin, spin a coin,
　All fall down;
Queen Nefertiti
　Stalks through the town.

Over the pavements
　Her feet go clack
Her legs are as tall
　As a chimney stack;

Her fingers flicker
　Like snakes in the air,
The walls split open
　At her green-eyed stare;

Her voice is thin
　As the ghosts of bees;
She will crumble your bones,
　She will make your blood freeze.

Spin a coin, spin a coin,
　All fall down;
Queen Nefertiti
　Stalks through the town.

Anonymous

Do You Ever Think?

Do you ever think when a hearse goes by
That you may be the next to die?
An undertaker tall and thin
Digs a hole and puts you in.
All goes well for about a week,
And then the coffin begins to leak.
The worms crawl in. The worms crawl out.
The worms play pinochle on your snout!
They use your bones for telephones
And call you up when you're not home.

Traditional American

Monster Stew

If you are getting tired
Of plain old witches' brew,
Next time you have a party
Try gourmet monster stew.

Put on an old black apron
Borrowed from a witch;
Then scoop in murky water
From a brackish ditch.

Pond slime is the next thing,
A bucketful or two;
But if you don't have pond slime,
Some moldy soup will do.

Now measure in an owl-hoot,
Two grumbles and a groan.
To make it really tasty,
Add an eerie moan.

Now if your guests are monsters,
You cackle while they eat.
They'll say your stew is gruesome,
A most delightful treat!

Judith Kinter

Song of the Witches

Double, double toil and trouble;
Fire burn and caldron bubble.
Fillet of a fenny snake,
In the caldron boil and bake;
Eye of newt and toe of frog,
Wool of bat and tongue of dog,
Adder's fork and blind-worm's sting,
Lizard's leg and howlet's wing,
For a charm of powerful trouble,
Like a hell-broth boil and bubble.

Double, double toil and trouble;
Fire burn and caldron bubble.
Cool it with a baboon's blood,
Then the charm is firm and good.

Macbeth: IV.i. 10–19; 35–38
William Shakespeare

The Witches' Charm

The owl is abroad, the bat and the toad,
   And so is the cat-a-mountain;
The ant and the mole sit both in a hole,
   And the frog peeps out o' the fountain.

from The Masque of Queens
Ben Jonson

The Owl

The dark grows tall
   Above the trees.
She will not stir
   Unless she sees
A rabbit sigh.
   She will not soar
Until she hears
   A mouse's roar.

J. Patrick Lewis

from Wanted — A Witch's Cat

Wanted — a witch's cat.
Must have vigor and spite,
Be expert at hissing,
And good in a fight,
And have balance and poise
On a broomstick at night.

Shelagh McGee

The Bat

By day the bat is cousin to the mouse.
He likes the attic of an aging house.

His fingers make a hat about his head.
His pulse beat is so slow we think him dead.

He loops in crazy figures half the night
Among the trees that face the corner light.

But when he brushes up against a screen,
We are afraid of what our eyes have seen:

For something is amiss or out of place
When mice with wings can wear a human face.

Theodore Roethke

Three Ghostesses

Three little ghostesses,
Sitting on postesses,
Eating buttered toastesses,
Greasing their fistesses,
Up to their wristesses,
Oh, what beastesses,
To make such feastesses!

Anonymous

Look at That!

Look at that!
Ghosts lined up
at the laundromat,
all around the
block.

Each has
bleach
and some
detergent.

Each one seems to
think it
urgent

to take a spin
in a
washing machine

before the
clock
strikes
Halloween!

Lilian Moore

The Cemetery Stones

The cemetery stones are walking
in the final shadows of the light,
white beneath the village stars,
tilting away to night.

George Mendoza

Skeleton Parade

The skeletons are out tonight,
They march about the street
With bony bodies, bony heads
And bony hands and feet.

Bony bony bony bones
With nothing in between
Up and down and all around
They march on Halloween.

Jack Prelutsky

Pumpkin

After its lid
Is cut, the slick
Seeds and stuck
Wet strings
Scooped out,
Walls scraped
Dry and white,
Face carved, candle
Fixed and lit,
Light creeps
Into the thick
Rind: giving
That dead orange
Vegetable skull
Warm skin, making
A live head
To hold its
Sharp gold grin.
          Valerie Worth

The Witches' Ride

Over the hills
Where the edge of the light
Deepens and darkens
To ebony night,
Narrow hats high
Above yellow bead eyes,
The tatter-haired witches
Ride through the skies.
Over the seas
Where the flat fishes sleep
Wrapped in the slap of the slippery deep,
Over the peaks
Where the black trees are bare,
Where bony birds quiver
They glide through the air.
Silently humming
A horrible tune,
They sweep through the stillness
To sit on the moon.

Karla Kuskin

When I'm Very Nearly Sleeping

When I'm very nearly sleeping
in the middle of the night,
and I hear the furtive creeping
of a thing that likes to bite,
you may be completely certain
that I haven't any fear,
though when it is on the curtain,
how I wish it were not here.

When I sense the creature perching
on my pillow underneath,
and suspect that it is searching
for a spot to sink its teeth,
when I'm sure I feel it flitting
but an inch above my head,
I am glad a lamp is sitting
on the table by my bed.

Jack Prelutsky